How Owls Become Wise

Written by Kelly Partridge

Illustrated by Stephanie Hider

This book is dedicated to anyone who has ever
been the victim of bullying.
Know that you are perfect just as you are.

It was Olivia Owl's first day of school in her new town. She was happy to make new friends and learn how to hunt. She waved goodbye to her father and flew to her classroom.

When she was inside, Olivia saw all of the owls watching their teacher. Mrs. Gray was teaching the owls how to catch food. At the end of the lesson, she planned to take the class outside to show them how to catch a mouse.

Mrs. Gray introduced Olivia to the class and told her to take a seat. Olivia, being a barn owl, flew over to the other barn owls and sat down. They quickly became friends, introducing themselves as Sophie, James, and Dennis. Olivia was so happy to have new friends already. As they talked, Olivia could not help but notice one lonely owl sitting in the back of the room by himself.

Mrs. Gray took the class into the forest to show them how to hunt. The young owls sat on a tree, leaving the one lonely owl alone on a branch.

Olivia asked, "How come that owl is by himself?"

Sophie laughed. "That is Nick. We do not talk to him."

"Why doesn't anyone want to talk to Nick?" Olivia asked.

Sophie giggled. "Do you see him, Olivia?

He is wearing glasses! What type of owl wears glasses?"

Dennis loudly asked, "How will he be able to hunt with glasses? He cannot even see!"

James flew over to Nick, and with one claw, he pulled Nick's glasses from his beak. They fell to the ground.

Nick flew into a thornbush as he tried to pick up his glasses. The class laughed and pointed as he pulled himself from the thornbush. Olivia felt guilty laughing at Nick, but she wanted her new friends to like her, so she laughed too.

Mrs. Gray flew down to grab Nick's broken glasses from the ground and scolded the class for their mean actions. Olivia knew that laughing at Nick was wrong, so she was the first to stop.

When class ended, Olivia saw Nick flying behind the rest of the class.

His feathers were messy, and his wing was hurt from flying into the thornbush. Olivia wanted to stand up for Nick, but she did not want to be teased, so she said nothing.

The next day at school, Nick sat
in the back of the room by himself.
His glasses were taped together.

The snowy owls saw Nick with his broken
glasses and yelled, "Nick the nerd. Nick the nerd."
Soon the entire class joined in.
Olivia did not join in at first, but mean glances
from Dennis, James, and Sophie caused
Olivia to start chanting too. Olivia could tell
Nick's feelings were hurt, but her new friends
were smiling at her, so she said nothing.

As they were eating lunch
that day, Olivia kept glancing
at Nick, who was eating alone.

Sophie poked Olivia in the side.
"Do you want to be friends
with Nick the nerd?"

"No, I just feel sorry for him. He is always alone," Olivia replied.

"Do not feel sorry for him," Dennis said.

"Yeah. You do not want to be seen with him, do you?" James asked.

"No, I guess not," Olivia said. She hated to say that,
but her answer pleased her friends,
        and they stopped bugging her.

At recess, most of the young owls were playing on the playground. Nick sat alone on a tree branch, reading his book. Olivia, Sophie, James, and Dennis played a game of catch. Olivia, wanting to impress her new friends, yelled to Dennis,

"Go long."

She threw the ball over Dennis's head and right at Nick. The ball hit his book and knocked it to the ground, where it landed in a puddle of mud. The owls laughed as Nick flew down to grab his dirty book.

When the bell rang, all of the owls flew back to class. As Olivia looked back at Nick, she saw him crying. She knew what she had done was wrong. Olivia wanted to apologize, but was afraid of what her friends would say. She stayed quiet and followed the others back inside.

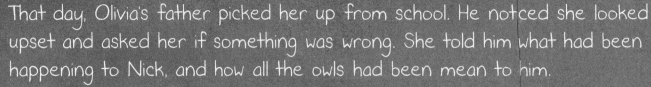

That day, Olivia's father picked her up from school. He notced she looked upset and asked her if something was wrong. She told him what had been happening to Nick, and how all the owls had been mean to him.

Looking at Olivia, her father asked,
"Well, what have you done when the other owls bully Nick?"

HA HA! HA HA!

Olivia looked at her father, puzzled. "Dad, we are not bullying Nick."

"Olivia, any time you pick on an owl for the way they look or act, for being different, or for the things they can and cannot do, you are bullying them. It is not okay to treat others this way. How would you feel if the class was picking on you?"

Olivia frowned. "I would not like it at all."

Her father asked, "When you see bad things happening to Nick, what do you do?"

Olivia admitted, "I laughed too, and today I threw a ball at him."

"Your mother and I taught you to be better than that. If you know it is wrong to bully another owl, and you can see it is hurting Nick's feelings, why are you a part of this?" her father said.

Olivia frowned. "I wanted to fit in."

Olivia's father frowned too and said, "Olivia, you do not have to bully Nick or anyone else to fit in. If the other owls at school pick on you for being nice to Nick, then they are not who you should be friends with."

Olivia hung her head in shame, and was quiet the rest of the way home.

Olivia knew her father was right. She tossed and turned in bed that night, thinking about what her father had said. She had known her actions were wrong all along, but she had continued to bully Nick to fit in.

With her father's words echoing in her head, she felt braver. She made up her mind right then to change her ways and not worry about what her classmates thought. She knew she needed to do something nice for Nick. After a while, Olivia thought of the perfect thing to do. Only then did she relax enough to feel sleepy. Tomorrow was going to be better, she thought as she closed her eyes.

The next day, Olivia put her favorite book in her backpack. As her father dropped her off at school, she kissed him goodbye and told him she would treat Nick better.

Olivia flew into the classroom and sat right next to Nick. The entire class stopped and stared at her. Nick looked startled and eyed her suspiciously. Olivia took a breath, forced herself to ignore the stares, and said, "Hi, Nick, my name is Olivia. I am very sorry I have been laughing at you and ruined your book."

Then she handed him the book from her backpack. "This is my favorite story, and I want to share it with you. I would like to be friends, if that is okay with you."

Nick smiled and nodded.

At recess, Olivia started a game of tag with Nick. Olivia was soon having so much fun that ignoring the stares she felt from the rest of the class was easy. Her classmates' angry stares turned to looks of longing to join in. Sophie, James, and Dennis were the first to fly over, and Olivia became worried. Was she going to be bullied too? Sophie and Dennis stayed behind James and would not make eye contact with Olivia or Nick.

James nervously stammered, "We were wondering, I mean, uh, would you let us play too?" Olivia smiled with relief as she and Nick nodded. Soon after, the entire class was laughing and playing tag together.

When the bell rang, all the owls flew back to class together. Olivia sat down next to Nick. So did Sophie, James, and Dennis. Olivia smiled to herself as she saw the positive impact her actions had made on her friends.

Olivia's father picked her up from school that day. Olivia was so happy with how the day had gone, and she could not wait to tell her father about it.

Her father smiled at her and said, "I'm proud of you for sticking up for what you know is right. You saw you were part of a bad situation, and you changed your actions. You were willing to admit you were wrong, say you were sorry, and learn from your mistake. Your bravery to make the first move caused a positive change in your classmates. This is how you will one day become a wise owl!"

Olivia smiled proudly at her father's praise.

The next day when Olivia flew into the classroom, she saw Nick was already sitting with Sophie, Dennis, and James. Nick had saved Olivia a seat right next to him. As Olivia sat down, Nick reached into his backpack and handed her something.

"What is it?" Olivia asked.

"It is my new favorite story," Nick said as he handed her the book she had let him borrow him yesterday.

Olivia smiled. "You finished it already?"

Nick nodded happily. "I couldn't put it down."

Olivia and Nick smiled at their new friends as they talked and laughed while they waited for class to start.

Talk About It

1. What is bullying?

2. How do you think other people who are bullied feel?

3. Have you every tried to help someone that you saw being bullied? If yes, what happened?

4. What is something positive you could do next time you witness someone being bullied?

5. What could you do if you are bullied?

6. What adults do you trust to get help with bullying?

About the Author

Kelly Partridge is the founder of Contribution Clothing LLC, a mission driven online boutique with a focus on female empowerment and community support. She is passionate about social justice issues, and received her Masters of Science in Nonprofit Management and Philanthropy from Bay Path University. She currently resides in Ludlow, Massachusetts with her dog Lucy and partner. This is her first children's book, and it has been a lifelong dream of hers to become a published author.

Learn more about Kelly and her story at www.contributionclothing.com

CPSIA information can be obtained
at www.ICGtesting.com
Printed in the USA
BVHW011521120421
604731BV00003B/222